GOSCINNY AND UDERZO
PRESENT
An Asterix Adventure

OBELIX
& CO.

Written by RENÉ GOSCINNY *and Illustrated by* ALBERT UDERZO

Translated by Anthea Bell *and* Derek Hockridge

© 1976 GOSCINNY/UDERZO

Revised edition and English translation © 2004 HACHETTE

Original title: *Obélix et compagnie*

Exclusive licensee: Orion Publishing Group
Translators: Anthea Bell and Derek Hockridge
Typography: Bryony Newhouse

This revised edition first published in Great Britain by Orion Publishing Group

This paperback edition first published in 2004 by Orion Books Ltd,
Orion House, 5 Upper Saint Martin's Lane, London WC2H 9EA
An Hachette Livre UK Company

7 9 10 8 6

Printed in France by Qualibris

http://gb.asterix.com
www.orionbooks.co.uk

A CIP record for this book is available from the British Library

ISBN 978 0 7528 6651 2 (cased)
ISBN 978 0 7528 6652 9 (paperback)

Distributed in the United States of America by Sterling Publishing Co. Inc.
387 Park Avenue South, New York, NY 10016

The Orion Publishing Group's policy is to use papers that are natural, renewable and recyclable products
and made from wood grown in sustainable forests. The logging and manufacturing processes are
expected to conform to the environmental regulations of the country of origin.

GAULISH VILLAGE

COMPENDIUM

LAUDANUM

AQUARIUM

TOTORUM

ARMORICA

BELGICA

LUTETIA

GAUL
(ROMAN CONQUEST)
50 BC

CELTICA

AQUITANIA

PROVINCIA

THE YEAR IS 50 BC. GAUL IS ENTIRELY OCCUPIED BY THE
ROMANS. WELL, NOT ENTIRELY ... ONE SMALL VILLAGE OF
INDOMITABLE GAULS STILL HOLDS OUT AGAINST THE INVADERS.
AND LIFE IS NOT EASY FOR THE ROMAN LEGIONARIES WHO
GARRISON THE FORTIFIED CAMPS OF TOTORUM, AQUARIUM,
LAUDANUM AND COMPENDIUM ...

ASTERIX, THE HERO OF THESE ADVENTURES. A SHREWD, CUNNING LITTLE WARRIOR, ALL PERILOUS MISSIONS ARE IMMEDIATELY ENTRUSTED TO HIM. ASTERIX GETS HIS SUPERHUMAN STRENGTH FROM THE MAGIC POTION BREWED BY THE DRUID GETAFIX . . .

OBELIX, ASTERIX'S INSEPARABLE FRIEND. A MENHIR DELIVERY MAN BY TRADE, ADDICTED TO WILD BOAR. OBELIX IS ALWAYS READY TO DROP EVERYTHING AND GO OFF ON A NEW ADVENTURE WITH ASTERIX – SO LONG AS THERE'S WILD BOAR TO EAT, AND PLENTY OF FIGHTING. HIS CONSTANT COMPANION IS DOGMATIX, THE ONLY KNOWN CANINE ECOLOGIST, WHO HOWLS WITH DESPAIR WHEN A TREE IS CUT DOWN.

GETAFIX, THE VENERABLE VILLAGE DRUID, GATHERS MISTLETOE AND BREWS MAGIC POTIONS. HIS SPECIALITY IS THE POTION WHICH GIVES THE DRINKER SUPERHUMAN STRENGTH. BUT GETAFIX ALSO HAS OTHER RECIPES UP HIS SLEEVE . . .

CACOFONIX, THE BARD. OPINION IS DIVIDED AS TO HIS MUSICAL GIFTS. CACOFONIX THINKS HE'S A GENIUS. EVERY-ONE ELSE THINKS HE'S UNSPEAKABLE. BUT SO LONG AS HE DOESN'T SPEAK, LET ALONE SING, EVERYBODY LIKES HIM . . .

FINALLY, VITALSTATISTIX, THE CHIEF OF THE TRIBE. MAJESTIC, BRAVE AND HOT-TEMPERED, THE OLD WARRIOR IS RESPECTED BY HIS MEN AND FEARED BY HIS ENEMIES. VITALSTATISTIX HIMSELF HAS ONLY ONE FEAR, HE IS AFRAID THE SKY MAY FALL ON HIS HEAD TOMORROW. BUT AS HE ALWAYS SAYS, TOMORROW NEVER COMES.

DISCIPLINE IS FAIRLY LAX IN THE FORTIFIED ROMAN CAMP OF TOTORUM...

IT'S OUR RELIEF, BOYS! IT'S OUR RELIEF!

OPEN THE GATES! OPEN THE GATES!

HEY, CENTURION SCROFULUS! IT'S THEM ALL RIGHT!

I AM CENTURION IGNORAMUS! AVE!

HI! I'M CENTURION SCROFULUS... AVE! WHAT A RELIEF!

NOT IN UNIFORM, CENTURION SCROFULUS?

WE HARDLY EVER GO OUT, SO WE DON'T BOTHER TO DRESS UP.

SCRATCH SCRATCH

FORWARD MARCH!

I LIKE A NICE MARCH PAST, I DO!

EH?

A WORD OF ADVICE... TAKE IT EASY AND WAIT FOR YOUR RELIEF. AND IGNORE ANY PROVOCATION FROM THE LOCAL GAULS. THEY'RE CRAZY. THEY'RE ALSO INVINCIBLE.

I HAVE EVERY INTENTION OF BRINGING THOSE VERY GAULS TO HEEL! THAT WILL PLEASE JULIUS CAESAR... AND I DON'T WANT TO STAY A CENTURION MY WHOLE LIFE LONG!

SOUNDS LIKE YOUR WHOLE LIFE WON'T BE LONG... WELL, GET MOVING, LADS!

IN ROME...

ONE MAN! ONE SOLITARY GAUL MANAGED TO DEFEAT AND DEMORALISE MY CRACK TROOPS!

THIS IS TOO MUCH! THESE GAULS MAKE ME LOOK RIDICULOUS. WE CAN'T GO ON LIKE THIS, BY JUPITER! WELL? I'M WAITING FOR SUGGESTIONS!

WE COULD SEND THE ENTIRE ARMY...

YES, BUT WE MUSTN'T LEAVE OUR FRONTIERS UNGUARDED.

SUPPOSE WE SET UP A COMMISSION TO STUDY THE PROBLEM?

GOOD IDEA! WITH SUB-COMMITTEES TO CONSIDER THE VARIOUS ASPECTS...

LET'S HAVE A WORKING LUNCH TO DISCUSS IT...

TAPTAPTAP! TAPTAP!

THEY ARE STRONG, SO WE MUST WEAKEN THEM. THEY HAVE NOTHING TO DO BUT FIGHT, SO WE MUST KEEP THEM BUSY SOME OTHER WAY...

8A

COME HERE, CAIUS PREPOSTERUS. JUST HOW WOULD YOU SET ABOUT WEAKENING THE GAULS, WITH THEIR MAGICAL STRENGTH?

GO ON! LET'S SEE WHAT THEY TAUGHT YOU AT THE LATIN SCHOOL OF ECONOMICS...

EASY, O CAESAR. GOLD, THE PROFIT MOTIVE...

...WILL ENFEEBLE THEM AND KEEP THEM BUSY. WE MUST CORRUPT THEM.

YOU THINK THAT WILL DO THE TRICK?

LOOK AROUND YOU, O CAESAR!

8B

SEVERAL DAYS LATER, IN THE CAMP OF TOTORUM...

YES, HE'S A FAT MAN. OFTEN GOES FOR WALKS WITH A MENHIR ON HIS BACK AND A LITTLE DOG AT HIS HEELS...

YOU MIGHT WELL RUN INTO HIM IN THE FOREST... SO WATCH OUT! EVEN THE LITTLE DOG IS DANGEROUS.

I'M OFF. YOU MEN, DON'T LEAVE CAMP?

NOT LIKELY! WE'RE NOT LEAVING TILL WE'RE RELIEVED.

SOON AFTERWARDS...

PICKED UP A SCENT? LET'S HAVE A LOOK...

GRRRRRR!

?

OH, HOW BEAUTIFUL! JUST LOOK WHAT'S BEHIND YOU!

BEHIND ME?

BUT THERE ISN'T ANYTHING BEHIND ME!

YES, THERE IS! THAT MENHIR!

OH YES, I FORGOT... IT'S ONLY A MENHIR.

?

MAGNIFICENT!

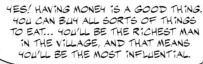

OH, HOW BEAUTIFUL, ANALGESIX! JUST LOOK WHAT'S BEHIND YOU!

?

IT'S ONLY A BOAR!

I KNOW IT'S A BOAR, YOU FOOL. LET ME HAVE IT!

ARE YOU CRAZY?

TAP! TAP! TAP.

HERE. YOU CAN USE THIS TO BUY THINGS, AND THEN YOU'LL BE THE SECOND RICHEST MAN IN THE VILLAGE.

AND I'LL BUY ALL YOU CAN DELIVER.

???

TOMORROW I'LL PAY YOU TWO HANDFULS OF COINS, BECAUSE PRICES ARE TROTTING THROUGH THE MARKET PLACE AND GETTING BLOWN UP IN THE AIR, AND IT'S ALL RATHER COMPLICATED.

!!!

DINNER TIME, ANALGESIX!

I CAN'T STOP! I'VE GOT WORK TO DO!

?!

IT'S THE MENHIR DELIVERY MAN!

EIGHT HUNDRED SESTERTII.

YOU MEAN MORE PRICES HAVE BEEN CANTERING THROUGH THE MARKET PLACE SINCE YESTERDAY?

EH?... OH, YES, BUT THERE'S A SLIGHT PROBLEM. YOU'RE ONLY BRINGING ME ONE MENHIR AT A TIME, AND I NEED LOTS OF MENHIRS...

I CAN'T MAKE THEM ANY FASTER. I CAN ONLY MAKE ONE A DAY BECAUSE I FELL INTO THE CAULDRON OF MAGIC POTION AS A BABY...

WHAT A PITY...

IF YOU CAN'T INCREASE THE EFFICIENCY OF YOUR PRODUCTIVITY INFRASTRUCTURE, THE MARKET WILL FALL.

UH?

IF YOU NOT ABLE MAKE BIG HEAP MENHIRS, ME NOT ABLE PAY HEAP BIG SESTERTII. YOU SAVVY?

ASTERIX, COULD YOU HELP ME MAKE MENHIRS?

?

YOU SEE, IF THE INFRA-STRUCTURE DOESN'T GALLOP FASTER THERE'LL BE HEAPS OF SESTERTII FALLING IN THE MARKET.

UH?

YOU SAVVY?

TAP! TAP! TAP!

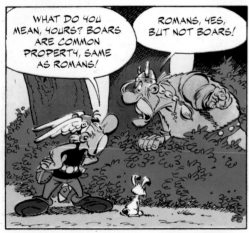

WHAT HAPPENED, BY TOUTATIS?

?

BIG HEAP SKY FALL ON OUR HEADS!

LET'S HAVE A WORD WITH OBELIX!

OBELIX QUARRY

CAUTION MENHIRS TURNING

CERTAINLY NOT... THE MENHIR BUSINESS HAS NEVER HAD IT SO GOOD. I'M GETTING TO BE THE MOST INFLUENTIAL MAN IN THE VILLAGE.

ARE YOU NUTS, OR WHAT?

OBELIX QUARRY
UTION MENHIRS TURNING

BUT WOULDN'T YOU RATHER HUNT BOAR AND HAVE FUN WITH YOUR FRIENDS, LIKE YOU USED TO?

OF COURSE. WHEN I'VE SOLD HEAPS OF MENHIRS I'LL BE ABLE TO HUNT BOAR AGAIN...

COME ON, DOGMATIX! THE MOST INFLUENTIAL MAN IN THE VILLAGE! HUH!

COME AND WORK FOR ME, ASTERIX, AND IN A FEW YEARS WE'LL BE.....

OUCH!

DOGMATIX BIT ME!

I DON'T THINK IT'S ANYTHING SERIOUS...

BUT WHAT BOTHERS ME IS THIS SUDDEN PASSION THE ROMANS HAVE FOR MENHIRS...

NOT BAD GOING, BUT I MUST TALK TO YOU... I SUGGEST WE HAVE A WORKING LUNCH.

THAT'S LUCKY. SOMETHING SEEMS TO HAVE KEPT MY HUNTERS IN THE FOREST TODAY.

PRODUCTION HAS INCREASED, BUT YOU STILL HAVE A DELIVER PROBLEM. YOU NEED TO STEP UP THE EFFICIENCY OF YOUR DISTRIBUTION CHANNELS.

UH?

SORRY, I FORGOT... YOU NOT BRING PLENTY MENHIRS ALL ONE TIME. YOU BRING MORE MENHIRS QUICK QUICK!

ME NOT FIND PLENTY DELIVERY MEN...

WELL, THINK THE PROBLEM OVER. WE'LL BE IN TOUCH AND HAVE ANOTHER WORKING LUNCH.

AND ANOTHER THING: YOU WANT TO START SPENDING YOUR SESTERTII. YOU NEED SOME SMARTER CLOTHES...

WHY? WHAT'S THE MATTER WITH MY BREECHES?

IT'S NOT THE WAY FOR A MAN WHO'S DOING SO WELL IN MENHIRS TO DRESS.

IT ISN'T?

* LYONS
* AMIENS
* SWITZERLAND

BY JUPITER! LOOK AT THAT!

OBELIX & CO.

SPLENDID! WELL DONE! COME INTO MY TENT AND WE'LL GET DOWN TO BUSINESS. MENHIRS ARE GOING UP AGAIN.

BUT I HAVE TO UNLOAD MY MENHIRS...

NO, NO! THAT'S NO JOB FOR A CAPTAIN OF INDUSTRY.

OBELIX & CO.

UNLOAD THE MENHIRS, YOU LOT!

UH?

23A

UNLOAD HEAP BIG MENHIRS! YOU SAVVY?

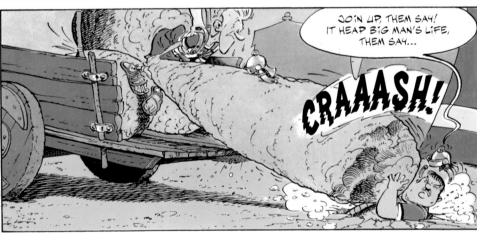

JOIN UP, THEM SAY! IT HEAP BIG MAN'S LIFE, THEM SAY...

CRAAASH!

SOON AFTERWARDS...

HULLO, OBELIX!

I JUST WANTED TO CONGRATULATE YOU ON BECOMING THE MOST INFLUENTIAL MAN IN THE VILLAGE.

YOU DID? ER... WELL...

BY THE WAY... YOU COULDN'T DO SOMETHING FOR ME, COULD YOU?

OF COURSE!

23B

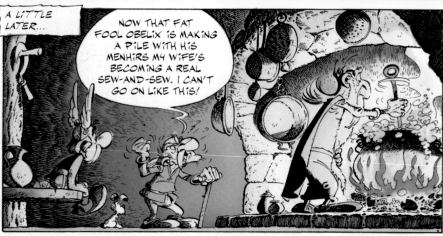

30

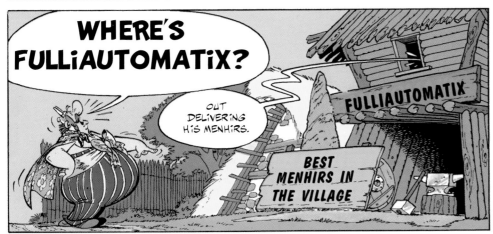

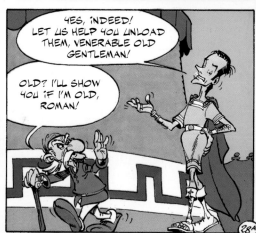

WHAT DOES THE CHIEF WANT US FOR?

WE'LL SOON SEE.

?

WHAT HAPPENED TO HIM?

HE WANTED TO WORK IN FULLIAUTOMATIX'S QUARRY, BUT FULLIAUTOMATIX DOESN'T CARE FOR MUSIC WHILE HE WORKS.

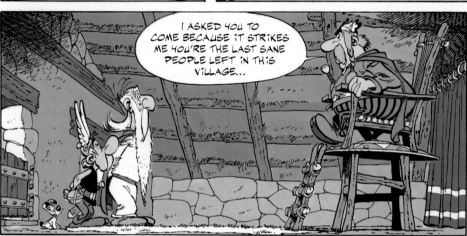

I ASKED YOU TO COME BECAUSE IT STRIKES ME YOU'RE THE LAST SANE PEOPLE LEFT IN THIS VILLAGE...

THEY'VE ALL GONE NUTS! HALF OF THEM ARE HUNTING BOAR TO FEED THE OTHER HALF, WHO ARE MAKING MENHIRS! WHAT ON EARTH IS ALL THIS IN AID OF?

DON'T WORRY, O CHIEF!

I'M NOT WORRIED...

...I'VE KNOWN THEY WERE ALL NUTS FOR AGES. BUT NOW IMPEDIMENTA KEEPS TELLING ME I OUGHT TO BE MAKING MENHIRS TOO...

...SAYS SHE CAN'T FACE HER FRIENDS THESE DAYS. THEIR HUSBANDS ARE ROLLING IN SESTERTII...

BE PATIENT...

THE ROMANS' TROUBLES AREN'T OVER. THEY'LL FIND US AND OUR MENHIRS TOUGH NUTS TO CRACK!

HOHOHO! HOHOHO!

HWARF! HWARF! HWARF!

SLAP! SLAP! SLAP!

NOW THEY'RE NUTS TOO!

IN JULIUS CAESAR'S PALACE IN ROME...

AND JUST WHAT AM I SUPPOSED TO DO WITH ALL THESE MENHIRS?

BUT CAESAR, THOSE MENHIRS ARE THE PROOF OF MY SUCCESS! THE GAULS ARE TOO BUSY MAKING MENHIRS TO FIGHT, SO...

MAYBE, BUT YOU'RE DRAINING MY TREASURY TO KEEP A FEW MADMEN BUSY!

PEACE IS BEYOND ALL PRICE... SI VIS PACEM...

YOUNG MAN, I MAKE THE CLASSICAL REMARKS AROUND HERE, ALEA JACTA EST AND ALL THAT, AND WHAT'S MORE, YOU HAVEN'T ANSWERED MY QUESTION: WHAT AM I SUPPOSED TO DO WITH ALL THESE MENHIRS?

SELL THEM, O CAESAR.

SELL THEM?

THAT'S RIGHT. THAT WAY, YOU NOT ONLY RECOVER YOUR EXPENSES, YOU MAKE A PROFIT TOO.

BUT WHO'D WANT MENHIRS? THEY'RE NO GOOD FOR ANYTHING!

PRECISELY! WE MUST DRAW UP A PLAN OF CAMPAIGN, DECIDE ON OUR STRATEGY, SET OUR SIGHTS ON THE RIGHT TARGET!

CAMPAIGN? STRATEGY? TARGET? THAT'S THE KIND OF THING I LIKE TO HEAR! I'LL GIVE ORDERS FOR THE LEGIONS TO PREPARE FOR BATTLE!

NO, NO! LET ME EXPLAIN...

THE FOLLOWING PASSAGE WILL BE DIFFICULT FOR THOSE OF YOU UNACQUAINTED WITH THE ANCIENT BUSINESS WORLD TO UNDERSTAND, ESPECIALLY AS, THESE DAYS, SUCH A STATE OF AFFAIRS COULD NEVER EXIST, SINCE NO ONE WOULD DREAM OF TRYING TO SELL SOMETHING UTTERLY USELESS...

AT THIS PRESENT MOMENT IN TIME THE DEMAND FOR MENHIRS IS VIRTUALLY NIL. THEREFORE WE MUST BE CREATIVE... FIND HOW TO APPEAL TO THE POTENTIAL CONSUMER...

LET US STUDY THOSE FACTORS WHICH WILL ALLOW US TO HOME IN ON OUR TARGET...

PEOPLE WILL BUY:
A: SOMETHING USEFUL;
B: SOMETHING COMFORTABLE;
C: SOMETHING THAT'S FUN;
D: SOMETHING TO MAKE THE NEIGHBOURS ENVIOUS.
WE HAVE TO AIM FOR D!

A CAMPAIGN CENTRED ON A CAREFULLY DEFINED AREA SHOULD ALLOW US TO MAKE RAPID CONTACT WITH A LARGE BODY OF CONSUMERS ABLE TO ABSORB OUR STOCKS AT MAXIMUM SPEED...

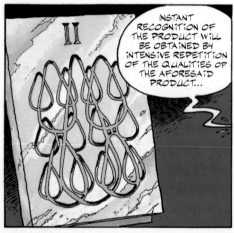

INSTANT RECOGNITION OF THE PRODUCT WILL BE OBTAINED BY INTENSIVE REPETITION OF THE QUALITIES OF THE AFORESAID PRODUCT...

...WHICH MAY BE DEFINED AS FOLLOWS:
A: DURABILITY;
B: SOLIDITY;
C: OTHER QUALITIES.

THUS I MAKE NO RASH PROMISES WHEN I SAY THAT WE SHOULD SUCCEED IN OBTAINING POSITIVE RESULTS, SALESWISE, AT NO VERY DISTANT DATE.

UH?

ME THINK YOU ABLE SELL HEAP BIG HEAP MENHIRS PLENTY QUICK.

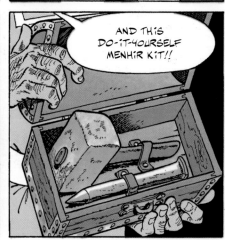

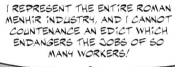

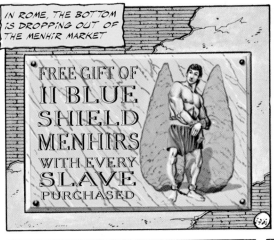

IN ROME, THE BOTTOM IS DROPPING OUT OF THE MENHIR MARKET

FREE GIFT OF II BLUE SHIELD MENHIRS WITH EVERY SLAVE PURCHASED

PEOPLE DON'T EVEN WANT THEM AS A GIFT... WELL, THAT'S TOO BAD! I'VE LOST A FORTUNE, BUT LET'S FORGET IT...

THE THING IS...

YES?

WELL, IT'S LIKE THIS, O CAESAR...

I WANTED TO KEEP THE PEACE IN GAUL, SO BEFORE I LEFT I GAVE ORDERS FOR THEM TO GO ON BUYING MENHIRS... AND RAISING THE PRICE.

WHAT? YOU KNOW THE STATE OF MY FINANCES? AND YOU SAID WE'D MAKE A KILLING! GET BACK TO GAUL AND STOP IT!!!

ER... YOU WOULDN'T LIKE TO SEND SOMEONE ELSE, WOULD YOU? I HAVE A FRIEND WHO WAS AT BUSINESS SCHOOL WITH ME. HE...

YOU'RE GOING YOURSELF, YOU IDIOT! IT'S YOUR FAULT I NEARLY HAD A CIVIL WAR ON MY HANDS! ROME MIGHT HAVE BEEN RUINED! EVEN BRUTUS HAS BEEN GIVING ME NASTY LOOKS!

BUT... BUT THEY'LL KILL ME!

THAT PARTICULAR KILLING WOULDN'T WORRY ME!

ANYWAY, IF YOU DON'T GO I'LL HAVE YOU THROWN TO THE LIONS!!

MENHIR GRAVEYARD

BUT THE WORLD MENHIR CRISIS HAS NOT YET AFFECTED THE GAULISH VILLAGE...

ASTERIX! DOGMATIX!

?!

LISTEN... CAN I GO HUNTING BOARS WITH YOU?

38A

WHAT, AN INFLUENTIAL MAN LIKE YOU? DON'T YOU HAVE A CONFERENCE? DON'T YOU HAVE A BUSINESS LUNCH?

PLEASE DON'T LAUGH AT ME. I KNOW I'VE BEEN SILLY. I'M BORED, AND I'VE HAD ENOUGH! EVERYONE HAS LOTS OF SESTERTII NOW! EVERYONE'S THE MOST INFLUENTIAL MAN IN THE VILLAGE!

I WANT TO BE FRIENDS AGAIN! I WANT TO HUNT BOAR! I WANT TO HAVE FUN... BOOOHOOO!

WERE YOU THINKING OF HUNTING BOARS IN THAT GET-UP?

SNIFF... HMPH?

I'LL BE RIGHT BACK!

TEEHEE!

38B

THE CAMP OF TOTORUM...

HEY, WHAT DO YOU KNOW? OLD PREPOSTERUS IS BACK!

AVE, PREPOSTERUS! I CARRIED OUT YOUR ORDERS; WE HAVE VAST STOCKS OF MENHIRS...

AND I HOPE YOU'VE BROUGHT PLENTY OF SESTERTII, BECAUSE...

WATCH OUT, YOU LOT, HERE COMES ANOTHER CLOWN!

UNHYGIENIX

FRESH MENHIRS

HERE ARE SOME MORE MENHIRS. YOUR LEGIONARIES CAN UNLOAD THEM.

NO. TAKE THEM AWAY!

?!

WHAT?

I'M NOT BUYING ANY MORE MENHIRS.

BUT WHAT AM I GOING TO DO WITH THEM...? SUPPOSE I LET YOU HAVE THEM CHEAP?

NOOOOO!

NO MORE MENHIRS! GET OUT!

WELL, HONESTLY!

I DON'T KNOW THAT I UNDERSTAND YOUR NEW STRATEGY...

THERE ISN'T ANY STRATEGY. WE'RE NOT BUYING ANY MORE MENHIRS, THAT'S ALL!

RIGHT! I'LL BE OFF. AVE!

?!

OH NO, YOU WON'T! YOU'RE STAYING HERE UNTIL I FULLY UNDERSTAND THE SITUATION!

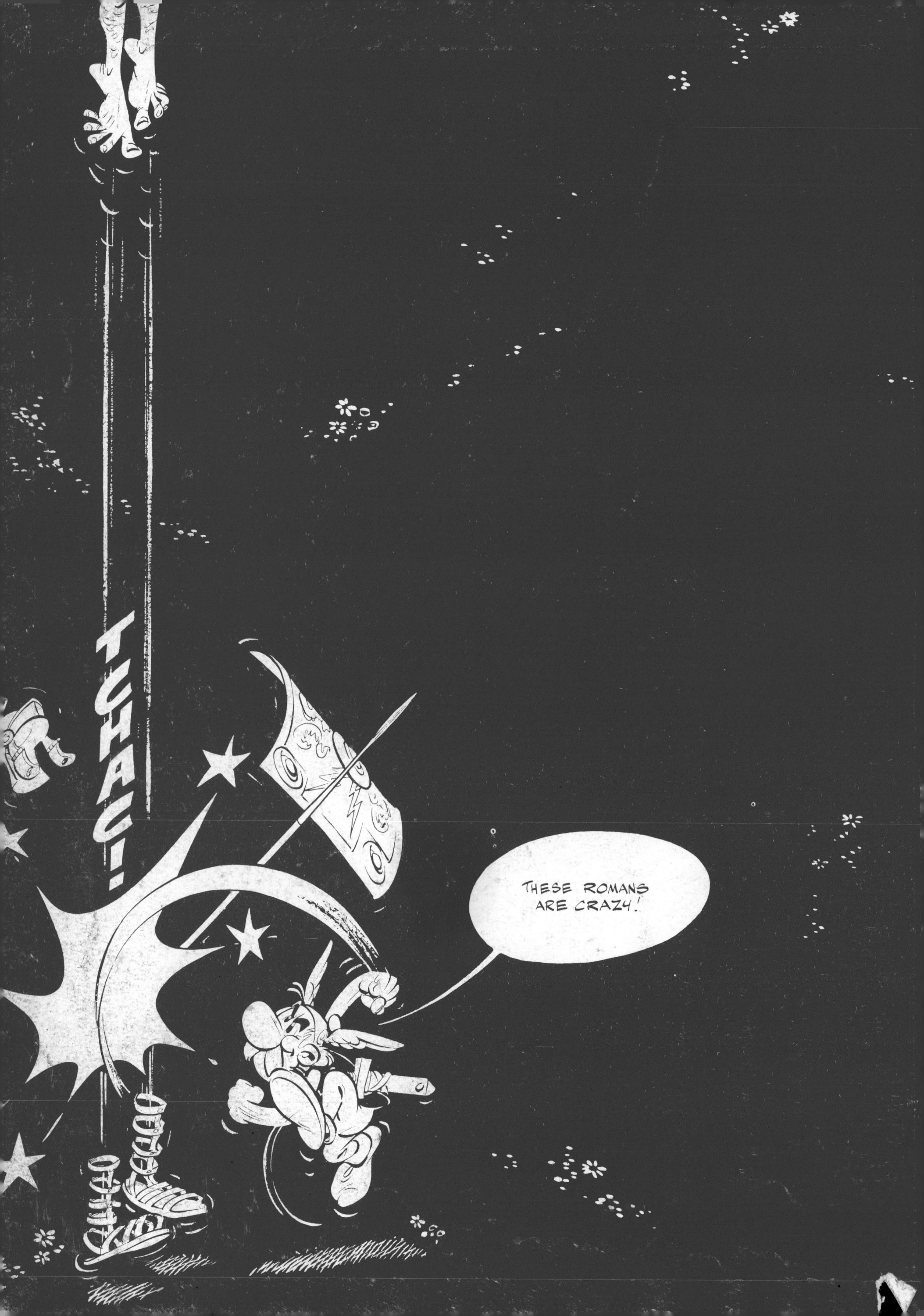
THWACK!
THESE ROMANS ARE CRAZY!